SKIPPY AND OAF
THE BATTLE AGAINST OXYGEN RADICALS

BY
CRAIG S. COUSINEAU

DNA Press™
©2007

Library of Congress Cataloging-in-Publication Data
Cousineau, Craig. Skippy and Oaf : the battle against oxygen radicals /
Craig Cousineau. —1st ed.   p. cm.
Summary: Skippy, who loves fruits and vegetables, teaches his fellow labrat, Oaf, who loves junk food, about the heroic actions of antioxidants as they battle evil oxygen radicals in the body.

ISBN 1-933255-27-7   (alk. paper)

[1. Nutrition—Fiction. 2. Food habits—Fiction. 3. Antioxidants—Fiction.
    4. Rats—Fiction.] I. Title. II. Title: Battle against oxygen radicals.
    PZ7.C831743Ski 2007
    [Fic]—dc22
    2 0 0 6 0 3 9 4 5 7

DNA Press, LLC
P.O. BOX 572
Eagleville, PA 19408, USA
www.dnapress.com
editors@dnapress.com

Publisher: DNA Press, LLC
Executive Editor: Alexander Kuklin
Art Direction: Alex Nartea
Cover Art: Mark Stefanowicz (www.markstef.com)
Illustrations: Nataliya Bellony (NBIllustration@aol.com)

To Cody and Eric Cousineau.

Table of Contents

LIFE IN THE LABORATORY

Early one Monday morning the alarm clock started to buzz. Skippy was already awake and jumped up to turn off the alarm.

"Wake up, Oaf!" Skippy shouted, "It's seven o'clock."

Oaf continued to snore loudly. The alarm never woke him up. Just like every other morning, Skippy had to give Oaf a shove to wake him up.

"All right, I'm up," Oaf muttered as he rolled out of bed. The smell of breakfast was the only thing that could lure Oaf out of bed. Skippy made his way to the kitchen and Oaf followed slowly behind.

"Good morning, you two, how are we this morning?" Dr. Jim asked as they walked in.

Skippy was quick to answer, "I feel great!"

"How about you, Oaf?"

Oaf's eyes were still half shut. A few seconds later he answered, "I'm starving. I haven't eaten since my midnight snack. Where's breakfast, Dr. Jim?"

"Almost done, Oaf." Dr. Jim said as he finished fixing the meals. Oaf waited at the table for his food, trying not to fall back asleep.

"That's right, Doc!" said Oaf as Dr. Jim put the plates on the table. "You know what I like." Oaf's eyes lit up at the sight of food.

His plate wasn't on the table a second before he tore into it. The hamburger, fries, eggs over easy and coffee were actually waking him up.

"Boy, Doc, this sure is good," Oaf said between mouthfuls. "What are you having Skippy?"

"A blueberry-banana smoothie, some oatmeal, and orange juice," Skippy answered, eating at a much slower pace than Oaf.

"What?" Oaf rarely ate any fruits or vegetables himself. "How could you eat that? It sounds terrible!"

"Now just hold on, Oaf. I think I can tell you a few things that will change your mind."

"No way! You'll never see me eating that stuff!" Oaf gave Skippy's breakfast a disgusted look.

"He's right, Oaf," said Dr. Jim as he walked out. "Explain a few things to him, Skippy. I have some experiments to do."

Skippy and Oaf lived with Dr. Jim in his lab. Lately, he had been trying to teach them some important things about fruits and vegetables. Skippy remembered everything he was taught, but Oaf barely listened to a word.

"What does he mean, Skippy? What could be so good about fruits and vegetables?" Oaf had barely tried any fruits or vegetables and he wasn't about to start.

"There's plenty of good things about them," Skippy said. "You hardly ever eat them, and you don't know how good many of them taste. You should really listen to what Dr. Jim's been teaching us. Do you think I eat fruits and vegetables just for fun?"

Oaf never took what Dr. Jim said about plant foods very seriously. He didn't believe it mattered if you ate them or not. He always chose sugary or greasy foods whenever Dr. Jim was cooking.

"Well, then, tell me what the big deal is with them; I'll listen," Oaf promised, even though he knew that whatever Skippy tried to teach him would only bore him until lunch time.

Oaf usually daydreamed about lunch during Dr. Jim's lessons.

WHAT DID CAVEMEN EAT?

Skippy barely knew where to start. There were so many things he'd learned about fruits and vegetables from Dr. Jim. "First off, besides tasting great and helping me keep in shape, they protect my DNA and provide my body with powerful antioxidants."

"Hold on!" Oaf said, with a very confused look on his face. "DNA? Antioxidants? What are you talking about?" Those words didn't mean a thing to him.

"Oh no," Skippy muttered. This was going to be harder than he thought. "I guess this will take a lot of explaining. We'll have to get back to DNA in a little bit. Okay, let's go way back. Think about humans that lived a long, long time ago. Cavemen, what did they eat?"

Oaf had to think for a few seconds. "Whatever they could find, I suppose. Mostly plants they found growing, maybe a little hunting."

"That's right, they were gatherers and hunters. Plants were a much bigger part of their diet than meat."

Oaf didn't see what Skippy was getting at. "Mostly vegetables? I'm sure glad I wasn't around then!"

"What do you think happened after thousands of years of eating mostly plants?"

"I don't have a clue, Skippy. I don't even

want to think about it!"

They were just getting done with breakfast. Skippy was finishing his juice and Oaf was making sure he devoured every last crumb on his plate.

Skippy was getting a little frustrated with the way Oaf refused to learn anything new. "Well then, I'll tell you," he said. "They ate so many plants for so long their bodies depended on getting enough of them every day, and they still do."

"You can stop right there, Skippy! You're not fooling anyone. You're saying that human bodies depend on plant foods. We're rats, Skippy, nice try. We don't have to worry about all this!"

Skippy let out a sigh. He was trying not to get too angry at Oaf. "You can't just eat bacon double

cheeseburgers every day."

We have a long way to go here. Come on, let's go for a walk."

"No! I'm still tired. I only got 10 hours of sleep! Can't we just sit down?" Oaf pleaded. He rarely had much energy.

Skippy made Oaf get up, but he moved slowly so Oaf could keep up with him. Oaf had to use a cane to get around. On top of not eating well, he hardly ever exercised.

DNA - THE MAGIC CODE

"I know I've been talking about humans, but you have no idea how similar we are to them," said Skippy. "That means you need to understand DNA."

"Similar to humans?" Oaf said. "I don't think so. Anyone can see that we're not at all alike!"

"Calm down, Oaf. DNA is hard to explain, so try and understand. Walk a little faster, too. You shouldn't have eaten so much!"

"I can't help it. Dr. Jim whips up a real good breakfast. Beats that junk you eat."

"Just wait Oaf, I know I'll change your mind."

They started to walk around the lab as Skippy geared up for what he knew was going to be some difficult explaining.

"DNA," Skippy began, "is found in every single tiny cell in our bodies. It's in the form of a

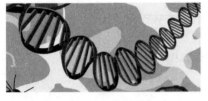 very long strand."

Skippy continued, "Each strand is made up of these tiny little things called 'bases'. There are four different bases: A, T, C, and G. These bases connect in millions of different combinations. The different combinations of bases in our DNA are what make us all look different."

"What do those letters stand for?" asked Oaf, showing a little interest.

"Well," Skippy started, having a little trouble

remembering the names, "I think Dr. Jim said that A, T, C, and G stand for adenine, thymine, cytosine, and guanine."

"That's going to be hard to remember," Oaf thought to himself. He still was having trouble catching on.

"How do those combinations work to make us look different?" he asked.

"The letters, or bases, are the code that tells your cells what proteins to make. The code for

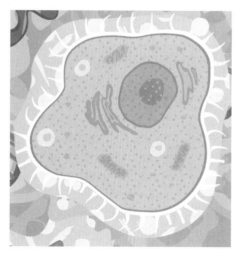

a protein can be anywhere from about thirty to hundreds of bases long."

Skippy explained, "How long the code for a protein is depends on how small or big the protein being made is. Proteins make up the parts of our bodies and help them grow. They do important things inside our bodies like make sure all of our cells have enough oxygen and break down the food we eat. In fact, proteins take care of most of the things our bodies need to do to stay alive."

"That doesn't sound too hard to under- stand," said Oaf. "What else do I need to know about DNA?"

"Unless you have an identical twin, your DNA is different from everyone else's in the world. That's why everyone looks different. My eyes are blue and your eyes are brown because we each have our own unique DNA code."

Oaf remembered hearing all of this in one of Dr. Jim's lessons, and it was starting to make sense now. "Alright, I get this. DNA is in all of my cells and controls what proteins my cells make. Proteins make up my body and do most of the important stuff inside of it."

RATS AND HUMANS

Skippy was pleased that there was hope for Oaf after all. "That's as simple as I can explain it. I guess we can sit for a while," Skippy said. Oaf looked like he needed a little break. "There's a lot more to learn, though. Now that you understand DNA, the next step is to learn what makes rats and humans similar."

Even after learning about DNA, Oaf was still suspicious. He just couldn't see any possible way rats and humans could be alike. "There's just no way Skippy, you can't fool me. I know what you and Dr. Jim are up to!"

"Just relax, Oaf. Next you have to understand what a 'genome' is. Your DNA controls everything about you. The color of your eyes, your height, what color your fur is, and all of the things going on inside of your body are decided by the code in your DNA. Each and every one of the proteins your body makes has its own code. A string of bases that codes for a protein, like the kind your hair is made out of, is called a gene. Your genome, then..."

"Wait, wait!" Oaf interrupted. "A what?" Oaf asked. "A jean? Like the kind we wear?"

"No, no," Skippy chuckled. "These genes are spelled g-e-n-e-s, and they're very different from the jeans you're wearing."

"Okay then. So the codes for proteins in DNA are called genes. What's a genome then?" Oaf asked.

"It's pretty simple. Think of it this way: if genes are like words in a book, then your genome is the book that makes you. Genome is just a fancy name for all of your genes put together." Skippy explained.

"So each gene makes a different protein, and all the genes put together is called a genome. Your genome is like a big instruction manual that makes you?" Oaf asked.

"Exactly," said Skippy. "Pretty simple isn't it?"

"Yeah, it is. I get everything so far. But you still haven't proven to me how we're similar to humans."

"You're being a little impatient Oaf, I'm getting to that. We should get up, you need to finish walking off all that breakfast you had."

Oaf lifted himself up and got beside Skippy for another walk. He was starting to think all this stuff was pretty interesting and that he wasn't as bored as he thought he would be. He was also starting to wish he wasn't so tired all the time.

OXYGEN RADICALS ATTACK!

Skippy could tell Oaf was getting interested. "Now think about this," he said. "Do you think Dr. Jim would work with us in the lab if what he found out wasn't important to humans?"

"Well, no. I guess that wouldn't make sense." Oaf felt silly for never realizing this. "So what makes us alike?"

Skippy had the facts all ready to go. "The first thing is that a rat's genome isn't that much smaller than a human's genome. There are about 35,000 genes in a human's genome. That's more than in our genome, but not by much."

"How could that be? Humans are so much bigger than us!" Oaf yelled.

"Actually, the size of an animal doesn't have much affect on how big its genome is. Scientists have found that even some microscopic animals have larger genomes than humans."

Oaf was so amazed he couldn't think of anything to say. He was really regretting not listening to Dr. Jim more closely and thinking about lunch instead.

"Well, what else Skip?" Oaf asked.

"The next reason is the most important. Almost all diseases that are part of the human genome are part of our genome, too. That means that many of the diseases humans get can also affect us."

Just as Skippy finished the sentence, Dr. Jim walked in.

Oaf was amazed. "Oh, okay! So we help scientists solve serious diseases?"

Dr. Jim was happy to hear this. "That's right," he said. "Think of it this way. With your help, Oaf, maybe someday rats and humans can live without worrying about many of the diseases we have today!"

"Wow, this is great," Oaf said. "I didn't realize we were so important."

"Sounds like you're really learning, Oaf," said Dr. Jim. "You guys keep going and I'll see you at lunch. I hope you'll be ready to eat, Oaf!"

Usually Oaf got very excited when Dr. Jim said this, but first he wanted to keep learning all he could from Skippy. Oaf decided he was no longer bored. This stuff Skippy was telling him was really interesting.

"What's next, Skip?" Oaf asked.

"Now that you understand DNA well enough, I've got some bad news. Our DNA can get damaged. It can happen to anyone and can be very harmful," Skippy said in an eerie voice.

"What? Damaged?" said Oaf, worried. "How? If DNA is so small, how could it get harmed?"

Skippy could tell he really had Oaf's attention. "It can happen pretty easily and the cause is going to shock you."

Oaf could hardly wait for the answer. "Well? What is it?"

"The answer is...oxygen," answered Skippy,

still speaking eerily.

"What? No! How can that be? We breathe oxygen," Oaf stammered as he held his breath in a desperate attempt to protect his DNA.

"Yes, Oaf, oxygen. In the air you and I breathe. Do you want to know how it happens and how to stop it?"

Oaf wouldn't speak, he was too afraid to breathe.

"Now Oaf, holding your breath won't help!"

Oaf let out a loud gasp, he couldn't hold it any longer anyway. "I thought oxygen was good! Tell me how to stop it!" Oaf had completely forgotten about lunch. All he was worried about was his DNA.

"This is easier to understand than DNA. When we breathe, because of how hot it is in our bodies, the oxygen molecules split apart and become what are called 'oxygen radicals'," Skippy said, still using his eerie voice.

This sounded dangerous to Oaf. "Radicals, that doesn't sound good at all."

"That's right," Skippy began. "When an oxygen molecule splits apart in your body, it gets bad. They become oxygen radicals and inside your body cause tiny explosions that you can't feel.

 They can blow up and kill an entire cell, DNA and all. That's not even the worst part."

"What could be worse?" Oaf asked.

"Well, they can get inside your cells and damage just the DNA. Oxygen radicals can remove bases so they are no longer part of your code. Or they can switch bases around and change the code that way. DNA can fix itself, but not all the time. If oxygen radicals change your code and the DNA can't fix itself fast enough, the cell could mutate into a cancer cell, and the cancer could then multiply."

Oaf listened to all of this, looking horrified. "So oxygen radicals kill cells and can even cause cancer? How can we stop them?"

"Do you really want to know?" Skippy teased.

"What can we do?" Oaf pleaded. "I need to know!"

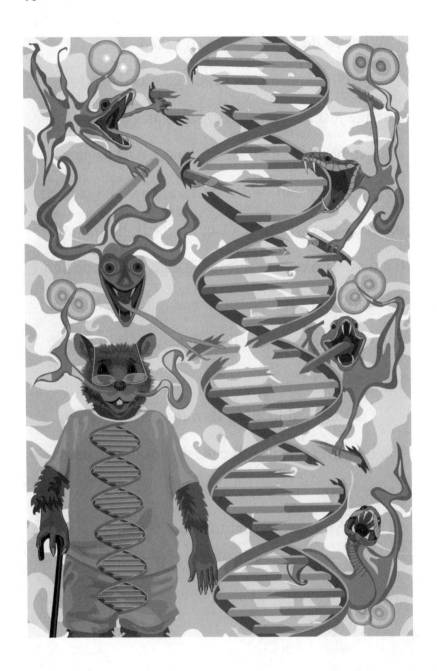

"It's simple, Oaf. Eat fruits and vegetables."

Hearing this, Oaf became suspicious. "No way, Skippy, you think you can fool me that easily? Fruits and vegetables? What do they have to do with DNA?"

Skippy wasn't about to give up. "Think for a second, Oaf," he said. "Plants are alive, just like we are. Oxygen radicals should hurt plants too, right?"

Oaf was surprised he had never realized this before. "Yeah, I guess they should. So then how do plants protect themselves?" Oaf asked.

"I'll tell you in a second. But first, tell me what makes apples red, carrots orange, and bananas yellow?"

As little as Oaf liked eating fruits and

vegetables, he knew why they all had their own colors.

"That's an easy one, Skip. Plants have what are called pigments. Pigments absorb and reflect different colors in the light spectrum. Apples absorb orange, yellow, green, blue, indigo, and violet light. But they reflect red light to our eyes."

"Good," Skippy was very pleased. "That's true, but did you know that pigments do more than just absorb and reflect light?"

Once again, Oaf was at a loss. "No, I didn't know that," he answered.

"Pigments also act as antioxidants," Skippy replied.

"Do you expect me to know what that word means?" Oaf asked feeling down.

"It's okay, Oaf," Skippy said. "Let's just break down the word. You know what anti means, right?"

Oaf thought he did. "Anti? It means against, right?"

"Yes it does," Skippy said. "Now the second part, 'oxidant', oxi, is oxygen."

"I got it! Antioxidant means against oxygen!" Oaf exclaimed as he figured it out.

"There you go, Oaf, that's right. Plants have chemicals that do two things. They're pigments that decide what color the plant will be and they're antioxidants that block harmful oxygen radicals from attacking cells. Just like Superheroes!"

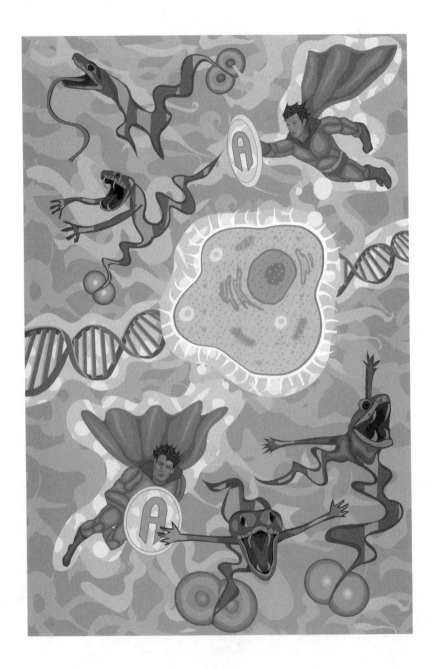

ANTIOXIDANT SUPERHEROES

"Come with me, I know an experiment that will help explain this."

Skippy and Oaf made their way into the kitchen. Going into the kitchen made Oaf think of his all time favorite hobby, eating. He hadn't thought about lunch in a while, and now he was getting hungry. But, instead of opening a bag of chips he decided he would listen to what Skippy had to say next.

Skippy went to the counter and picked up an apple.

"This apple has a tough red skin," Skippy

began. "Watch what happens when we cut it in half."

They waited a few minutes. Oaf eyed up a bag of dill pickle chips until something about the sliced apple caught his attention.

"Hey, look at that! The apple is turning brown. Why is that, Skip?"

"Well, you now know that the red skin contains the pigments, or antioxidants. The white part of the apple doesn't have many, and without them the oxygen radicals are allowed to damage and burn the cells, so they turn brown."

After seeing the experiment, Oaf understood antioxidants. "I get it! Without antioxidants there's no protection from oxygen. That only took a few minutes, too! That scares me about what could be happening inside my body."

Oaf thought for a few seconds, then asked, "Can I have some of that apple?"

Oaf didn't remember the last time he had eaten any fruit, but now it seemed like a good idea.

"Do our bodies have their own antioxidants?" Oaf asked.

As Oaf began to chomp on the apple, Skippy replied, "Some, but not enough."

"Not enough? So our bodies can't protect themselves from oxygen alone? I suppose I should have the rest of that apple."

Skippy handed him the apple and was glad his lesson was working. "No they can't."

"Okay now, remember what I told you earlier about ancient humans?"

It took a few seconds for Oaf to remember. "Oh yeah, you said they ate so many plants their bodies depended on getting enough of them."

"Can you figure out why their bodies needed them?" Skippy challenged Oaf.

Oaf had really been listening and thought about his answer. "My guess would be that eating so many plants gave their bodies so many antioxidants they didn't worry about their cells being damaged or getting any bad diseases like cancer."

"That's the answer I was looking for," said Skippy. "But get this, because they ate so many plants, that could actually mean trouble for us."

"How could that be?" Oaf asked as he finished the apple.

"Well, after so many years of eating plants, their bodies didn't need to make as many antioxidants.

"Their bodies only made a few, while most of them came from their diets."

Oaf picked up another apple. "So their bodies used to make antioxidants, but since they ate so many plants, their bodies stopped making as many?"

"That's right, and that goes for us, too," said Skippy as he snacked on a juicy orange. "Our bodies don't make enough antioxidants either. We don't have enough chemicals made by our bodies to protect our DNA without the help of plants. DNA can't fix itself fast enough. If enough DNA damage builds up over time, bad things happen. Mutations can be very harmful, and even lead to cancer."

Moving on to his third apple, Oaf said, "So, we need enough antioxidants to keep up with DNA damage. And we can get them from the foods we eat, which should be plenty of fruits and vegetables!"

"You're a genius, Oaf. You got it!"

DNA REPAIR SYSTEM

"Well, Skippy, there's just one more question I have before we eat lunch," said Oaf, still hungry despite three apples.

"All right, Oaf, go ahead. I don't think Dr. Jim will make lunch for a few more minutes."

"I just ate three apples. I know the antioxidants help me, but how does my body actually use them?"

Oaf had asked a very good question, and Skippy was ready with an answer. "There are two ways, and both depend on eating the right foods. The first thing our body does is store antioxidants right when we eat them. They line up on the surface of our organs and go right to work fighting off oxygen radicals."

"And what's the second way?" Oaf was excited to know.

"Once again, when we eat the right foods, we get antioxidants from them. They trigger our body to produce 'enzymes' that help eat up oxygen radicals."

This was simple enough for Oaf to understand right away. "So when I ate the apple, the antioxidants started blocking oxygen radicals right away. They also help my body make enzymes that get rid of oxygen radicals?"

"Yes, that's all correct. Now remember, it's important to always have antioxidants in our body

so that our DNA has enough time to fix itself if any damage does happen. Plants are even more important as we get older. Our DNA repair system stops working very well and we need antioxidants to get rid of the oxygen that builds up in our cells."

"Or else our DNA can mutate and cause big problems!" Oaf added.

Dr. Jim walked into the kitchen just as Oaf added onto the end of Skippy's lesson. "Sounds like you have learned a lot today, Oaf."

"Sure have, Doc. Say, is it lunch time yet?"

"Yes, it is. What would you like today?" Dr. Jim asked.

"Well, let's see. Why don't you make me whatever Skippy is having?"

"That's great Oaf," Skippy said.

"I was hoping you would make that decision."

Dr. Jim was as pleased as Skippy was.

"I'm glad you finally caught on. How were those apples?"

CHICKEN AND HIS FRIENDS LEARN HOW YOU GET AND PREVENT THE FLU

By Amy Plouff

ISBN 1-933255-39-0

• Chicken and his friends will help children and their parents understand the science behind influenza (the flu) and the immune system in an accessible and entertaining way.

• Why would Chicken and his friends be able to do this?

• Chicken gets sick because he does not follow the advice of his teachers and parents. However, Doctor Parker explains how influenza viruses change, and how our immune system may not be able to recognize the new virus. Chicken and his friends learn how they can protect themselves through hand washing, learning the correct way to sneeze, social distancing (staying away from people when they're sick) and getting a flu vaccine.

"This book is one of the best science education books I have seen. The writing and illustrations are delightful, entertaining and good science."

Dr. Ralph Cordell,
Centers for Disease Control (CDC) Education Team, Division of Partnerships and Strategic Alliances, National Center for Health Marketing.

CHICKEN AND HIS FRIENDS LEARN HOW TO PREPARE FOR A PANDEMIC AND OTHER EMERGENCIES

By Amy Plouff

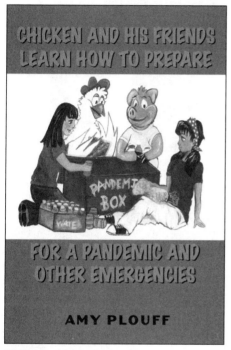

ISBN 1-933255-40-4

Chicken and his three best friends, two little girls and a pig, already know a lot about the science of preventing influenza (the flu). When they learn about the possibility of a pandemic, they decide to help their families prepare.

This book provides important information based on recommendations from the Centers for Disease Control and Prevention (CDC), and the U.S. Department of Health and Human Services in a format that is educational and fascinating. By understanding practical steps they can take, children and parents will find this book reassuring. Children will also learn about other times of crisis when Americans planted "Victory Gardens" and women like "Rosie the Riveter" worked in factories. Creative drawings and playful text explain the science behind preparing for a pandemic. Children and adults will love the interactions between Chicken and his friends.